TIMBUCTOO
GROWL

A sort of tiger from Timbuctoo

a story by
Roger Hargreaves

© Mrs Roger Hargreaves 1999
Published in Great Britain by Egmont World Ltd.,
Deanway Technology Centre, Wilmslow Road, Handforth,
Cheshire, SK9 3FB.
Printed in Italy
ISBN PBK 0 7498 4346 2
ISBN HBK 0 7498 4416 7

GROWL was a sort of tiger.
A Timbuctoo Tiger.

He lived in Stripe Cottage,
on the island of Timbuctoo.

Now you probably think that all
tigers are fierce, don't you?

Not **GROWL**. Not a bit.

He was the Timidest Tiger in the World!

It was a beautiful summer morning in Timbuctoo.

The sun was shining brightly, and **GROWL** was out for his morning walk.

Suddenly, out of the corner of his eye, **GROWL** noticed something following him.

He stopped.

Whatever it was that was following him stopped too.

OOOOOOOOOOHHHHHHHH!

GROWL took a deep, quivery breath.

"Who's there?" he asked in a little quivery voice.

"Who's there?"

No reply.

QUIVVVERRRRRR!

GROWL took a small step.
So too did whatever it was that was following him.

GROWL took a bigger step.
So too did whatever it was that was following him.

"Oh," cried **GROWL** timidly.
"Oh, help!"

And he ran away as fast as ever his legs could carry him.

And so too did whatever it was that was following him.

HELLLLLLLLLP!

GROWL ran and ran and ran right into Trumpet.

TRUMPET was a sort of elephant.

"Save me," cried **GROWL**, and he leapt into Trumpet's arms.

Trumpet stood there, holding **GROWL**, looking puzzled.

TRRRRRRUMPET!

"Why, **GROWL**," he said, "whatever is the matter?"

"There's something chasing me!" cried **GROWL** timidly.

"Where?" asked Trumpet, looking around.

"It's gone now," said **GROWL**, also looking around. "You can put me down!"

Trumpet put **GROWL** down.

"Oh, there it is again!!" shrieked
GROWL in terror.

And he jumped back into
Trumpet's arms.

Trumpet laughed a deep elephant-like laugh down his trunk.

"You silly tiger," he said. "Do you know what it was you were running away from?"

GROWL shook his head.

"Your shadow," chuckled Trumpet. "You've been running away from your own shadow!"

GROWL looked at him.
"Do shadows bite?" he asked timidly.

Trumpet chuckled again, and explained to **GROWL** that shadows only ever do what you do.

"Really, **GROWL**," he said. "You are the Timidest Tiger in the World!"

GROWL went on his way, much relieved.

"Silly old shadow," he said, looking over his shoulder.

Soon **GROWL** came to a pond.

Feeling a little thirsty, with all that running about, he went over to the pond to take a drink.

But, as he bent down to take a drink from the pond, he suddenly stopped.

SIP, SIP, SIP, SIP!

And jumped backwards.

And fell over.

And got up.

And ran away from that pond even faster than his legs could carry him.

HELLLLLLLLP !

He ran all the way back to Trumpet,
and jumped back into his arms.

"Save me!" he cried.

"More shadows?" asked Trumpet.

"No, no," sobbed **GROWL** timidly.

"There's a fierce creature," he pointed,
"... in the pond!"

"Show me," said Trumpet.

And they went back to the pond together.

"Oh, **GROWL**," laughed Trumpet.
"Do you want to know what it was
you were frightened of?"

GROWL nodded.

Can you guess what it was he was
frightened of?

In the pond?

His own reflection!

Oh, **GROWL**.

You really are the Timidest Tiger
in the World!